Copyright, Henry Holt and Company

ROBERT FROST
From the original in plaster
by Aroldo Du Chêne

MOUNTAIN INTERVAL

By

ROBERT FROST

Author of "North of Boston"

ISBN: 978-93-5128-547-2

First Published in 1916
Indian Reprint in 2017

Published by

Kalpaz Publications
C-30, Satyawati Nagar,
Delhi – 110052
E-mail: kalpaz@hotmail.com
Website: kalpazpublications.com
Ph.: +91-9212142040

Courtesy: D.K. Agencies (P) Ltd. <docinfo@dkagencies.com>

Frost, Robert, 1874-1963, **author.**
Mountain interval / by Robert Frost.
pages cm
Poems.
"First published in 1916"—Title page verso.
ISBN 9789351285472

1. American poetry. I. Title.

PS3511.R94M68 2017 DDC 811.52 23

TO YOU

WHO LEAST NEED REMINDING

that before this interval of the South Branch under black mountains, there was another interval, the Upper at Plymouth, where we walked in spring beyond the covered bridge; but that the first interval of all was the old farm, our brook interval, so called by the man we had it from in sale.

CONTENTS

CONTENTS

THE ROAD NOT TAKEN

Two roads diverged in a yellow wood,
And sorry I could not travel both
And be one traveler, long I stood
And looked down one as far as I could
To where it bent in the undergrowth;

Then took the other, as just as fair,
And having perhaps the better claim,
Because it was grassy and wanted wear;
Though as for that the passing there
Had worn them really about the same,

And both that morning equally lay
In leaves no step had trodden black.
Oh, I kept the first for another day!
Yet knowing how way leads on to way,
I doubted if I should ever come back.

I shall be telling this with a sigh
Somewhere ages and ages hence:
Two roads diverged in a wood, and I—
I took the one less traveled by,
And that has made all the difference.

CHRISTMAS TREES

(A Christmas Circular Letter)

THE city had withdrawn into itself
And left at last the country to the country;
When between whirls of snow not come to lie
And whirls of foliage not yet laid, there drove
A stranger to our yard, who looked the city,
Yet did in country fashion in that there
He sat and waited till he drew us out
A-buttoning coats to ask him who he was.
He proved to be the city come again
To look for something it had left behind
And could not do without and keep its Christmas.
He asked if I would sell my Christmas trees;
My woods — the young fir balsams like a place
Where houses all are churches and have spires.
I hadn't thought of them as Christmas Trees.
I doubt if I was tempted for a moment
To sell them off their feet to go in cars
And leave the slope behind the house all bare,
Where the sun shines now no warmer than the moon.
I'd hate to have them know it if I was.
Yet more I'd hate to hold my trees except
As others hold theirs or refuse for them,
Beyond the time of profitable growth,
The trial by market everything must come to.
I dallied so much with the thought of selling.

Then whether from mistaken courtesy
And fear of seeming short of speech, or whether
From hope of hearing good of what was mine,
I said, "There aren't enough to be worth while."
"I could soon tell how many they would cut,
You let me look them over."

"You could look.
But don't expect I'm going to let you have them."
Pasture they spring in, some in clumps too close
That lop each other of boughs, but not a few
Quite solitary and having equal boughs
All round and round. The latter he nodded "Yes" to,
Or paused to say beneath some lovelier one,
With a buyer's moderation, "That would do."
I thought so too, but wasn't there to say so.
We climbed the pasture on the south, crossed over,
And came down on the north.
He said, "A thousand."

"A thousand Christmas trees! — at what apiece?"

He felt some need of softening that to me:
"A thousand trees would come to thirty dollars."

Then I was certain I had never meant
To let him have them. Never show surprise!
But thirty dollars seemed so small beside
The extent of pasture I should strip, three cents
(For that was all they figured out apiece),
Three cents so small beside the dollar friends

I should be writing to within the hour
Would pay in cities for good trees like those,
Regular vestry-trees whole Sunday Schools
Could hang enough on to pick off enough.
A thousand Christmas trees I didn't know I had!
Worth three cents more to give away than sell,
As may be shown by a simple calculation.
Too bad I couldn't lay one in a letter.
I can't help wishing I could send you one,
In wishing you herewith a Merry Christmas.

AN OLD MAN'S WINTER NIGHT

All out of doors looked darkly in at him
Through the thin frost, almost in separate stars,
That gathers on the pane in empty rooms.
What kept his eyes from giving back the gaze
Was the lamp tilted near them in his hand.
What kept him from remembering what it was
That brought him to that creaking room was age.
He stood with barrels round him — at a loss.
And having scared the cellar under him
In clomping there, he scared it once again
In clomping off; — and scared the outer night,
Which has its sounds, familiar, like the roar
Of trees and crack of branches, common things,
But nothing so like beating on a box.
A light he was to no one but himself
Where now he sat, concerned with he knew what,
A quiet light, and then not even that.
He consigned to the moon, such as she was,
So late-arising, to the broken moon
As better than the sun in any case
For such a charge, his snow upon the roof,
His icicles along the wall to keep;
And slept. The log that shifted with a jolt
Once in the stove, disturbed him and he shifted,
And eased his heavy breathing, but still slept.
One aged man — one man — can't fill a house,
A farm, a countryside, or if he can,
It's thus he does it of a winter night.

A PATCH OF OLD SNOW

THERE'S a patch of old snow in a corner
  That I should have guessed
Was a blow-away paper the rain
  Had brought to rest.

It is speckled with grime as if
  Small print overspread it,
The news of a day I've forgotten —
  If I ever read it.

IN THE HOME STRETCH

SHE stood against the kitchen sink, and looked
Over the sink out through a dusty window
At weeds the water from the sink made tall.
She wore her cape; her hat was in her hand.
Behind her was confusion in the room,
Of chairs turned upside down to sit like people
In other chairs, and something, come to look,
For every room a house has — parlor, bed-room,
And dining-room — thrown pell-mell in the kitchen.
And now and then a smudged, infernal face
Looked in a door behind her and addressed
Her back. She always answered without turning.

"Where will I put this walnut bureau, lady?"
"Put it on top of something that's on top
Of something else," she laughed. "Oh, put it where
You can to-night, and go. It's almost dark;
You must be getting started back to town."
Another blackened face thrust in and looked
And smiled, and when she did not turn, spoke gently,
"What are you seeing out the window, *lady?*"

"Never was I beladied so before.
Would evidence of having been called lady
More than so many times make me a ladv
In common law. I wonder."

"But I ask,
What are you seeing out the window, lady?"

"What I'll be seeing more of in the years
To come as here I stand and go the round
Of many plates with towels many times."

"And what is that? You only put me off."

"Rank weeds that love the water from the dish-pan
More than some women like the dish-pan, Joe;
A little stretch of mowing-field for you;
Not much of that until I come to woods
That end all. And it's scarce enough to call
A view."

"And yet you think you like it, dear?"

"That's what you're so concerned to know! You hope
I like it. Bang goes something big away
Off there upstairs. The very tread of men
As great as those is shattering to the frame
Of such a little house. Once left alone,
You and I, dear, will go with softer steps
Up and down stairs and through the rooms, and none
But sudden winds that snatch them from our hands
Will ever slam the doors."

"I think you see
More than you like to own to out that window."

"No; for besides the things I tell you of,
I only see the years. They come and go
In alternation with the weeds, the field,
The wood."

"What kind of years?"

"Why, latter years—
Different from early years."

"I see them, too.
You didn't count them?"

"No, the further off
So ran together that I didn't try to.
It can scarce be that they would be in number
We'd care to know, for we are not young now.
And bang goes something else away off there.
It sounds as if it were the men went down,
And every crash meant one less to return
To lighted city streets we, too, have known,
But now are giving up for country darkness."

"Come from that window where you see too much for me,
And take a livelier view of things from here.
They're going. Watch this husky swarming up
Over the wheel into the sky-high seat,
Lighting his pipe now, squinting down his nose
At the flame burning downward as he sucks it."

"See how it makes his nose-side bright, a proof
How dark it's getting. Can you tell what time
It is by that? Or by the moon? The new moon!
What shoulder did I see her over? Neither.
A wire she is of silver, as new as we
To everything. Her light won't last us long.
It's something, though, to know we're going to have her
Night after night and stronger every night
To see us through our first two weeks. But, Joe,
The stove! Before they go! Knock on the window;
Ask them to help you get it on its feet.
We stand here dreaming. Hurry! Call them back!"

"They're not gone yet."

"We've got to have the stove,
Whatever else we want for. And a light.
Have we a piece of candle if the lamp
And oil are buried out of reach?"
Again
The house was full of tramping, and the dark,
Door-filling men burst in and seized the stove.
A cannon-mouth-like hole was in the wall,
To which they set it true by eye; and then
Came up the jointed stovepipe in their hands,
So much too light and airy for their strength
It almost seemed to come ballooning up,
Slipping from clumsy clutches toward the ceiling.
"A fit!" said one, and banged a stovepipe shoulder.
"It's good luck when you move in to begin
With good luck with your stovepipe. Never mind,
It's not so bad in the country, settled down,
When people 're getting on in life. You'll like it."
Joe said: "You big boys ought to find a farm,
And make good farmers, and leave other fellows
The city work to do. There's not enough
For everybody as it is in there."
"God!" one said wildly, and, when no one spoke:
"Say that to Jimmy here. He needs a farm."
But Jimmy only made his jaw recede
Fool-like, and rolled his eyes as if to say
He saw himself a farmer. Then there was a French boy
Who said with seriousness that made them laugh,
"Ma friend, you ain't know what it is you're ask."
He doffed his cap and held it with both hands
Across his chest to make as 'twere a bow:
"We're giving you our chances on de farm."
And then they all turned to with deafening boots
And put each other bodily out of the house.
"Goodby to them! We puzzle them. They think —

I don't know what they think we see in what
They leave us to: that pasture slope that seems
The back some farm presents us; and your woods
To northward from your window at the sink,
Waiting to steal a step on us whenever
We drop our eyes or turn to other things,
As in the game 'Ten-step' the children play."

"Good boys they seemed, and let them love the city.
All they could say was 'God!' when you proposed
Their coming out and making useful farmers."

"Did they make something lonesome go through you?
It would take more than them to sicken you —
Us of our bargain. But they left us so
As to our fate, like fools past reasoning with.
They almost shook *me*."

"It's all so much
What we have always wanted, I confess
It's seeming bad for a moment makes it seem
Even worse still, and so on down, down, down.
It's nothing; it's their leaving us at dusk.
I never bore it well when people went.
The first night after guests have gone, the house
Seems haunted or exposed. I always take
A personal interest in the locking up
At bedtime; but the strangeness soon wears off."
He fetched a dingy lantern from behind
A door. "There's that we didn't lose! And these!"—
Some matches he unpocketed. "For food —
The meals we've had no one can take from us.
I wish that everything on earth were just
As certain as the meals we've had. I wish

The meals we haven't had were, anyway.
What have you you know where to lay your hands on?"

"The bread we bought in passing at the store.
There's butter somewhere, too."

"Let's rend the bread.
I'll light the fire for company for you;
You'll not have any other company
Till Ed begins to get out on a Sunday
To look us over and give us his idea
Of what wants pruning, shingling, breaking up.
He'll know what he would do if he were we,
And all at once. He'll plan for us and plan
To help us, but he'll take it out in planning.
Well, you can set the table with the loaf.
Let's see you find your loaf. I'll light the fire.
I like chairs occupying other chairs
Not offering a lady —"

"There again, Joe!
You're tired."

"I'm drunk-nonsensical tired out;
Don't mind a word I say. It's a day's work
To empty one house of all household goods
And fill another with 'em fifteen miles away,
Although you do no more than dump them down."

"Dumped down in paradise we are and happy."

"It's all so much what I have always wanted,
I can't believe it's what you wanted, too."

"Shouldn't you like to know?"

"I'd like to know
If it is what you wanted, then how much
You wanted it for me."

"A troubled conscience!
You don't want me to tell if *I* don't know."

"I don't want to find out what can't be known.

But who first said the word to come?"

"My dear,
It's who first thought the thought. You're searching, Joe,
For things that don't exist; I mean beginnings.
Ends and beginnings—there are no such things.
There are only middles."

"What is this?"

"This life?
Our sitting here by lantern-light together
Amid the wreckage of a former home?
You won't deny the lantern isn't new.
The stove is not, and you are not to me,
Nor I to you."

"Perhaps you never were?"

"It would take me forever to recite
All that's not new in where we find ourselves.
New is a word for fools in towns who think
Style upon style in dress and thought at last
Must get somewhere. I've heard you say as much.
No, this is no beginning."

"Then an end?"

"End is a gloomy word."

"Is it too late
To drag you out for just a good-night call
On the old peach trees on the knoll to grope
By starlight in the grass for a last peach
The neighbors may not have taken as their right
When the house wasn't lived in? I've been looking:
I doubt if they have left us many grapes.
Before we set ourselves to right the house,
The first thing in the morning, out we go
To go the round of apple, cherry, peach,
Pine, alder, pasture, mowing, well, and brook.
All of a farm it is."

"I know this much:
I'm going to put you in your bed, if first
I have to make you build it. Come, the light."

When there was no more lantern in the kitchen,
The fire got out through crannies in the stove
And danced in yellow wrigglers on the ceiling,
As much at home as if they'd always danced there.

THE TELEPHONE

"WHEN I was just as far as I could walk
From here to-day,
There was an hour
All still
When leaning with my head against a flower
I heard you talk.
Don't say I didn't, for I heard you say —
You spoke from that flower on the window sill —
Do you remember what it was you said?"

"First tell me what it was you thought you heard."

"Having found the flower and driven a bee away,
I leaned my head,
And holding by the stalk,
I listened and I thought I caught the word —
What was it? Did you call me by my name?
Or did you say —
Someone said 'Come'— I heard it as I bowed."

"I may have thought as much, but not aloud."

"Well, so I came."

MEETING AND PASSING

As I went down the hill along the wall
There was a gate I had leaned at for the view
And had just turned from when I first saw you
As you came up the hill. We met. But all
We did that day was mingle great and small
Footprints in summer dust as if we drew
The figure of our being less than two
But more than one as yet. Your parasol

Pointed the decimal off with one deep thrust.
And all the time we talked you seemed to see
Something down there to smile at in the dust.
(Oh, it was without prejudice to me!)
Afterward I went past what you had passed
Before we met and you what I had passed.

HYLA BROOK

By June our brook's run out of song and speed.
Sought for much after that, it will be found
Either to have gone groping underground
(And taken with it all the Hyla breed
That shouted in the mist a month ago,
Like ghost of sleigh-bells in a ghost of snow)—
Or flourished and come up in jewel-weed,
Weak foliage that is blown upon and bent
Even against the way its waters went.
Its bed is left a faded paper sheet
Of dead leaves stuck together by the heat—
A brook to none but who remember long.
This as it will be seen is other far
Than with brooks taken otherwhere in song.
We love the things we love for what they are.

THE OVEN BIRD

THERE is a singer everyone has heard,
Loud, a mid-summer and a mid-wood bird,
Who makes the solid tree trunks sound again.
He says that leaves are old and that for flowers
Mid-summer is to spring as one to ten.
He says the early petal-fall is past
When pear and cherry bloom went down in showers
On sunny days a moment overcast;
And comes that other fall we name the fall.
He says the highway dust is over all.
The bird would cease and be as other birds
But that he knows in singing not to sing.
The question that he frames in all but words
Is what to make of a diminished thing.

BOND AND FREE

LOVE has earth to which she clings
With hills and circling arms about—
Wall within wall to shut fear out.
But Thought has need of no such things,
For Thought has a pair of dauntless wings.

On snow and sand and turf, I see
Where Love has left a printed trace
With straining in the world's embrace.
And such is Love and glad to be.
But Thought has shaken his ankles free.

Thought cleaves the interstellar gloom
And sits in Sirius' disc all night,
Till day makes him retrace his flight,
With smell of burning on every plume,
Back past the sun to an earthly room.

His gains in heaven are what they are.
Yet some say Love by being thrall
And simply staying possesses all
In several beauty that Thought fares far
To find fused in another star.

BIRCHES

WHEN I see birches bend to left and right
Across the lines of straighter darker trees,
I like to think some boy's been swinging them.
But swinging doesn't bend them down to stay.
Ice-storms do that. Often you must have seen them
Loaded with ice a sunny winter morning
After a rain. They click upon themselves
As the breeze rises, and turn many-colored
As the stir cracks and crazes their enamel.
Soon the sun's warmth makes them shed crystal shells
Shattering and avalanching on the snow-crust —
Such heaps of broken glass to sweep away
You'd think the inner dome of heaven had fallen.
They are dragged to the withered bracken by the load,
And they seem not to break; though once they are bowed
So low for long, they never right themselves:
You may see their trunks arching in the woods
Years afterwards, trailing their leaves on the ground
Like girls on hands and knees that throw their hair
Before them over their heads to dry in the sun.
But I was going to say when Truth broke in
With all her matter-of-fact about the ice-storm
(Now am I free to be poetical?)
I should prefer to have some boy bend them
As he went out and in to fetch the cows
Some boy too far from town to learn baseball,
Whose only play was what he found himself,
Summer or winter, and could play alone.
One by one he subdued his father's trees

By riding them down over and over again
Until he took the stiffness out of them,
And not one but hung limp, not one was left
For him to conquer. He learned all there was
To learn about not launching out too soon
And so not carrying the tree away
Clear to the ground. He always kept his poise
To the top branches, climbing carefully –
With the same pains you use to fill a cup
Up to the brim, and even above the brim.
Then he flung outward, feet first, with a swish,
Kicking his way down through the air to the ground.
So was I once myself a swinger of birches.
And so I dream of going back to be.
It's when I'm weary of considerations,
And life is too much like a pathless wood
Where your face burns and tickles with the cobwebs
Broken across it, and one eye is weeping
From a twig's having lashed across it open.
I'd like to get away from earth awhile
And then come back to it and begin over.
May no fate willfully misunderstand me
And half grant what I wish and snatch me away
Not to return. Earth's the right place for love:
I don't know where it's likely to go better.
I'd like to go by climbing a birch tree,
And climb black branches up a snow-white trunk
Toward heaven, till the tree could bear no more,
But dipped its top and set me down again.
That would be good both going and coming back.
One could do worse than be a swinger of birches.

PEA BRUSH

I WALKED down alone Sunday after church
  To the place where John has been cutting trees
To see for myself about the birch
  He said I could have to bush my peas.

The sun in the new-cut narrow gap
  Was hot enough for the first of May,
And stifling hot with the odor of sap
  From stumps still bleeding their life away.

The frogs that were peeping a thousand shrill
  Wherever the ground was low and wet,
The minute they heard my step went still
  To watch me and see what I came to get.

Birch boughs enough piled everywhere! —
  All fresh and sound from the recent axe.
Time someone came with cart and pair
  And got them off the wild flower's backs.

They might be good for garden things
  To curl a little finger round,
The same as you seize cat's-cradle strings,
  And lift themselves up off the ground.

Small good to anything growing wild,
  They were crooking many a trillium
That had budded before the boughs were piled
  And since it was coming up had to come.

PUTTING IN THE SEED

You come to fetch me from my work to-night
When supper's on the table, and we'll see
If I can leave off burying the white
Soft petals fallen from the apple tree.
(Soft petals, yes, but not so barren quite,
Mingled with these, smooth bean and wrinkled pea;)
And go along with you ere you lose sight
Of what you came for and become like me,
Slave to a springtime passion for the earth.
How Love burns through the Putting in the Seed
On through the watching for that early birth
When, just as the soil tarnishes with weed,

The sturdy seedling with arched body comes
Shouldering its way and shedding the earth crumbs.

A TIME TO TALK

When a friend calls to me from the road
And slows his horse to a meaning walk,
I don't stand still and look around
On all the hills I haven't hoed,
And shout from where I am, What is it?
No, not as there is a time to talk.
I thrust my hoe in the mellow ground,
Blade-end up and five feet tall,
And plod: I go up to the stone wall
For a friendly visit.

THE COW IN APPLE TIME

SOMETHING inspires the only cow of late
To make no more of a wall than an open gate,
And think no more of wall-builders than fools.
Her face is flecked with pomace and she drools
A cider syrup. Having tasted fruit,
She scorns a pasture withering to the root.
She runs from tree to tree where lie and sweeten
The windfalls spiked with stubble and worm-eaten.
She leaves them bitten when she has to fly.
She bellows on a knoll against the sky.
Her udder shrivels and the milk goes dry.

AN ENCOUNTER

ONCE on the kind of day called "weather breeder,"
When the heat slowly hazes and the sun
By its own power seems to be undone,
I was half boring through, half climbing through
A swamp of cedar. Choked with oil of cedar
And scurf of plants, and weary and over-heated,
And sorry I ever left the road I knew,
I paused and rested on a sort of hook
That had me by the coat as good as seated,
And since there was no other way to look,
Looked up toward heaven, and there against the blue,
Stood over me a resurrected tree,
A tree that had been down and raised again —
A barkless spectre. He had halted too,
As if for fear of treading upon me.
I saw the strange position of his hands —
Up at his shoulders, dragging yellow strands
Of wire with something in it from men to men.
"You here?" I said. "Where aren't you nowadays
And what's the news you carry — if you know?
And tell me where you're off for — Montreal?
Me? I'm not off for anywhere at all.
Sometimes I wander out of beaten ways
Half looking for the orchid Calypso."

RANGE-FINDING

THE battle rent a cobweb diamond-strung
And cut a flower beside a ground bird's nest
Before it stained a single human breast.
The stricken flower bent double and so hung.
And still the bird revisited her young.
A butterfly its fall had dispossessed
A moment sought in air his flower of rest,
Then lightly stooped to it and fluttering clung.

On the bare upland pasture there had spread
O'ernight 'twixt mullein stalks a wheel of thread
And straining cables wet with silver dew.
A sudden passing bullet shook it dry.
The indwelling spider ran to greet the fly,
But finding nothing, sullenly withdrew.

THE HILL WIFE

LONELINESS

(Her Word)

One ought not to have to care
So much as you and I
Care when the birds come round the house
To seem to say good-bye;

Or care so much when they come back
With whatever it is they sing;
The truth being we are as much
Too glad for the one thing

As we are too sad for the other here —
With birds that fill their breasts
But with each other and themselves
And their built or driven nests.

HOUSE FEAR

Always — I tell you this they learned —
Always at night when they returned
To the lonely house from far away
To lamps unlighted and fire gone gray,
They learned to rattle the lock and key
To give whatever might chance to be

Warning and time to be off in flight:
And preferring the out- to the in-door night,
They learned to leave the house-door wide
Until they had lit the lamp inside.

THE SMILE

(*Her Word*)

I didn't like the way he went away.
That smile! It never came of being gay.
Still he smiled — did you see him? — I was sure!
Perhaps because we gave him only bread
And the wretch knew from that that we were poor.
Perhaps because he let us give instead
Of seizing from us as he might have seized.
Perhaps he mocked at us for being wed,
Or being very young (and he was pleased
To have a vision of us old and dead).
I wonder how far down the road he's got.
He's watching from the woods as like as not.

THE OFT-REPEATED DREAM

She had no saying dark enough
  For the dark pine that kept
Forever trying the window-latch
  Of the room where they slept.

The tireless but ineffectual hands
  That with every futile pass
Made the great tree seem as a little bird
  Before the mystery of glass!

It never had been inside the room,
  And only one of the two
Was afraid in an oft-repeated dream
  Of what the tree might do.

THE IMPULSE

It was too lonely for her there,
  And too wild,
And since there were but two of them,
  And no child,

And work was little in the house,
  She was free,
And followed where he furrowed field,
  Or felled tree.

She rested on a log and tossed
  The fresh chips,
With a song only to herself
  On her lips.

And once she went to break a bough
  Of black alder.
She strayed so far she scarcely heard
  When he called her —

And didn't answer — didn't speak —
  Or return.
She stood, and then she ran and hid
  In the fern.

He never found her, though he looked
  Everywhere,
And he asked at her mother's house
  Was she there.

Sudden and swift and light as that
  The ties gave,
And he learned of finalities
  Besides the grave.

THE BONFIRE

" OH, let's go up the hill and scare ourselves,
As reckless as the best of them to-night,
By setting fire to all the brush we piled
With pitchy hands to wait for rain or snow.
Oh, let's not wait for rain to make it safe.
The pile is ours: we dragged it bough on bough
Down dark converging paths between the pines.
Let's not care what we do with it to-night.
Divide it? No! But burn it as one pile
The way we piled it. And let's be the talk
Of people brought to windows by a light
Thrown from somewhere against their wall-paper.
Rouse them all, both the free and not so free
With saying what they'd like to do to us
For what they'd better wait till we have done.
Let's all but bring to life this old volcano,
If that is what the mountain ever was —
And scare ourselves. Let wild fire loose we will. . ."

" And scare you too? " the children said together.

" Why wouldn't it scare me to have a fire
Begin in smudge with ropy smoke and know
That still, if I repent, I may recall it,
But in a moment not: a little spurt
Of burning fatness, and then nothing but
The fire itself can put it out, and that
By burning out, and before it burns out
It will have roared first and mixed sparks with stars,
And sweeping round it with a flaming sword,
Made the dim trees stand back in wider circle —

Done so much and I know not how much more
I mean it shall not do if I can bind it.
Well if it doesn't with its draft bring on
A wind to blow in earnest from some quarter,
As once it did with me upon an April.
The breezes were so spent with winter blowing
They seemed to fail the bluebirds under them
Short of the perch their languid flight was toward;
And my flame made a pinnacle to heaven
As I walked once round it in possession.
But the wind out of doors — you know the saying.
There came a gust. You used to think the trees
Made wind by fanning since you never knew
It blow but that you saw the trees in motion.
Something or someone watching made that gust.
It put the flame tip-down and dabbed the grass
Of over-winter with the least tip-touch
Your tongue gives salt or sugar in your hand.
The place it reached to blackened instantly.
The black was all there was by day-light,
That and the merest curl of cigarette smoke —
And a flame slender as the hepaticas,
Blood-root, and violets so soon to be now.
But the black spread like black death on the ground,
And I think the sky darkened with a cloud
Like winter and evening coming on together.
There were enough things to be thought of then.
Where the field stretches toward the north
And setting sun to Hyla brook, I gave it
To flames without twice thinking, where it verges
Upon the road, to flames too, though in fear
They might find fuel there, in withered brake,
Grass its full length, old silver golden-rod,
And alder and grape vine entanglement,
To leap the dusty deadline. For my own

I took what front there was beside. I knelt
And thrust hands in and held my face away.
Fight such a fire by rubbing not by beating.
A board is the best weapon if you have it.
I had my coat. And oh, I knew, I knew,
And said out loud, I couldn't bide the smother
And heat so close in; but the thought of all
The woods and town on fire by me, and all
The town turned out to fight for me — that held me.
I trusted the brook barrier, but feared
The road would fail; and on that side the fire
Died not without a noise of crackling wood —
Of something more than tinder-grass and weed —
That brought me to my feet to hold it back
By leaning back myself, as if the reins
Were round my neck and I was at the plough.
I won! But I'm sure no one ever spread
Another color over a tenth the space
That I spread coal-black over in the time
It took me. Neighbors coming home from town
Couldn't believe that so much black had come there
While they had backs turned, that it hadn't been there
When they had passed an hour or so before
Going the other way and they not seen it.
They looked about for someone to have done it.
But there was no one. I was somewhere wondering
Where all my weariness had gone and why
I walked so light on air in heavy shoes
In spite of a scorched Fourth-of-July feeling.
Why wouldn't I be scared remembering that?"

"If it scares you, what will it do to us?"

"Scare you. But if you shrink from being scared,
What would you say to war if it should come?

That's what for reasons I should like to know —
If you can comfort me by any answer."

"Oh, but war's not for children — it's for men."

"Now we are digging almost down to China.
My dears, my dears, you thought that — we all thought it.
So your mistake was ours. Haven't you heard, though,
About the ships where war has found them out
At sea, about the towns where war has come
Through opening clouds at night with droning speed
Further o'erhead than all but stars and angels,—
And children in the ships and in the towns?
Haven't you heard what we have lived to learn?
Nothing so new — something we had forgotten:
War is for everyone, for children too.
I wasn't going to tell you and I mustn't.
The best way is to come up hill with me
And have our fire and laugh and be afraid."

A GIRL'S GARDEN

A NEIGHBOR of mine in the village
  Likes to tell how one spring
When she was a girl on the farm, she did
  A childlike thing.

One day she asked her father
  To give her a garden plot
To plant and tend and reap herself,
  And he said, "Why not?"

In casting about for a corner
  He thought of an idle bit
Of walled-off ground where a shop had stood,
  And he said, "Just it."

And he said, "That ought to make you
  An ideal one-girl farm,
And give you a chance to put some strength
  On your slim-jim arm."

It was not enough of a garden,
  Her father said, to plough;
So she had to work it all by hand,
  But she don't mind now.

She wheeled the dung in the wheelbarrow
  Along a stretch of road;
But she always ran away and left
  Her not-nice load.

And hid from anyone passing.
  And then she begged the seed.
She says she thinks she planted one
  Of all things but weed.

A hill each of potatoes,
  Radishes, lettuce, peas,
Tomatoes, beets, beans, pumpkins, corn,
  And even fruit trees

And yes, she has long mistrusted
  That a cider apple tree
In bearing there to-day is hers,
  Or at least may be.

Her crop was a miscellany
  When all was said and done,
A little bit of everything,
  A great deal of none.

Now when she sees in the village
  How village things go,
Just when it seems to come in right,
  She says, "*I* know!

It's as when I was a farmer ——"
  Oh, never by way of advice!
And she never sins by telling the tale
  To the same person twice.

THE EXPOSED NEST

You were forever finding some new play.
So when I saw you down on hands and knees
In the meadow, busy with the new-cut hay,
Trying, I thought, to set it up on end,
I went to show you how to make it stay,
If that was your idea, against the breeze,
And, if you asked me, even help pretend
To make it root again and grow afresh.
But 'twas no make-believe with you to-day,
Nor was the grass itself your real concern,
Though I found your hand full of wilted fern,
Steel-bright June-grass, and blackening heads of clover.
'Twas a nest full of young birds on the ground
The cutter-bar had just gone champing over
(Miraculously without tasting flesh)
And left defenseless to the heat and light.
You wanted to restore them to their right
Of something interposed between their sight
And too much world at once — could means be found.
The way the nest-full every time we stirred
Stood up to us as to a mother-bird
Whose coming home has been too long deferred,
Made me ask would the mother-bird return
And care for them in such a change of scene
And might our meddling make her more afraid.
That was a thing we could not wait to learn.
We saw the risk we took in doing good,
But dared not spare to do the best we could
Though harm should come of it; so built the screen

You had begun, and gave them back their shade.
All this to prove we cared. Why is there then
No more to tell? We turned to other things.
I haven't any memory — have you? —
Of ever coming to the place again
To see if the birds lived the first night through,
And so at last to learn to use their wings.

"OUT, OUT —"

THE buzz-saw snarled and rattled in the yard
And made dust and dropped stove-length sticks of wood,
Sweet-scented stuff when the breeze drew across it.
And from there those that lifted eyes could count
Five mountain ranges one behind the other
Under the sunset far into Vermont.
And the saw snarled and rattled, snarled and rattled,
As it ran light, or had to bear a load.
And nothing happened: day was all but done.
Call it a day, I wish they might have said
To please the boy by giving him the half hour
That a boy counts so much when saved from work.
His sister stood beside them in her apron
To tell them "Supper." At the word, the saw,
As if to prove saws knew what supper meant,
Leaped out at the boy's hand, or seemed to leap —
He must have given the hand. However it was,
Neither refused the meeting. But the hand!
The boy's first outcry was a rueful laugh,
As he swung toward them holding up the hand
Half in appeal, but half as if to keep
The life from spilling. Then the boy saw all —
Since he was old enough to know, big boy
Doing a man's work, though a child at heart —
He saw all spoiled. "Don't let him cut my hand off —
The doctor, when he comes. Don't let him, sister!"
So. But the hand was gone already.
The doctor put him in the dark of ether.
He lay and puffed his lips out with his breath.

And then — the watcher at his pulse took fright.
No one believed. They listened at his heart.
Little — less — nothing! — and that ended it.
No more to build on there. And they, since they
Were not the one dead, turned to their affairs.

BROWN'S DESCENT

OR

THE WILLY-NILLY SLIDE

Brown lived at such a lofty farm
  That everyone for miles could see
His lantern when he did his chores
  In winter after half-past three.

And many must have seen him make
  His wild descent from there one night,
'Cross lots, 'cross walls, 'cross everything,
  Describing rings of lantern light.

Between the house and barn the gale
  Got him by something he had on
And blew him out on the icy crust
  That cased the world, and he was gone!

Walls were all buried, trees were few:
  He saw no stay unless he stove
A hole in somewhere with his heel.
  But though repeatedly he strove

And stamped and said things to himself,
  And sometimes something seemed to yield,
He gained no foothold, but pursued
  His journey down from field to field.

Sometimes he came with arms outspread
  Like wings, revolving in the scene
Upon his longer axis, and
  With no small dignity of mien.

Faster or slower as he chanced,
  Sitting or standing as he chose,
According as he feared to risk
  His neck, or thought to spare his clothes,

He never let the lantern drop.
  And some exclaimed who saw afar
The figures he described with it,
  " I wonder what those signals are

Brown makes at such an hour of night!
  He's celebrating something strange.
I wonder if he's sold his farm,
  Or been made Master of the Grange."

He reeled, he lurched, he bobbed, he checked;
  He fell and made the lantern rattle
(But saved the light from going out.)
  So half-way down he fought the battle

Incredulous of his own bad luck.
  And then becoming reconciled
To everything, he gave it up
  And came down like a coasting child.

"Well — I — be —" that was all he said,
  As standing in the river road,
He looked back up the slippery slope
  (Two miles it was) to his abode.

Sometimes as an authority
  On motor-cars, I'm asked if I
Should say our stock was petered out,
  And this is my sincere reply:

Yankees are what they always were.
  Don't think Brown ever gave up hope
Of getting home again because
  He couldn't climb that slippery slope;

Or even thought of standing there
  Until the January thaw
Should take the polish off the crust.
  He bowed with grace to natural law,

And then went round it on his feet,
  After the manner of our stock;
Not much concerned for those to whom,
  At that particular time o'clock,

It must have looked as if the course
  He steered was really straight away
From that which he was headed for —
  Not much concerned for them, I say;

No more so than became a man —
  And politician at odd seasons.
I've kept Brown standing in the cold
  While I invested him with reasons;

But now he snapped his eyes three times;
  Then shook his lantern, saying, "Ile's
'Bout out!" and took the long way home
  By road, a matter of several miles.

THE GUM-GATHERER

THERE overtook me and drew me in
To his down-hill, early-morning stride,
And set me five miles on my road
Better than if he had had me ride,
A man with a swinging bag for load
And half the bag wound round his hand.
We talked like barking above the din
Of water we walked along beside.
And for my telling him where I'd been
And where I lived in mountain land
To be coming home the way I was,
He told me a little about himself.
He came from higher up in the pass
Where the grist of the new-beginning brooks
Is blocks split off the mountain mass —
And hopeless grist enough it looks
Ever to grind to soil for grass.
(The way it is will do for moss.)
There he had built his stolen shack.
It had to be a stolen shack
Because of the fears of fire and loss
That trouble the sleep of lumber folk:
Visions of half the world burned black
And the sun shrunken yellow in smoke.
We know who when they come to town
Bring berries under the wagon seat,
Or a basket of eggs between their feet;
What this man brought in a cotton sack
Was gum, the gum of the mountain spruce.

He showed me lumps of the scented stuff
Like uncut jewels, dull and rough.
It comes to market golden brown;
But turns to pink between the teeth.

I told him this is a pleasant life
To set your breast to the bark of trees
That all your days are dim beneath,
And reaching up with a little knife,
To loose the resin and take it down
And bring it to market when you please.

THE LINE-GANG

HERE come the line-gang pioneering by.
They throw a forest down less cut than broken.
They plant dead trees for living, and the dead
They string together with a living thread.
They string an instrument against the sky
Wherein words whether beaten out or spoken
Will run as hushed as when they were a thought.
But in no hush they string it: they go past
With shouts afar to pull the cable taut,
To hold it hard until they make it fast,
To ease away — they have it. With a laugh,
An oath of towns that set the wild at naught
They bring the telephone and telegraph.

THE VANISHING RED

HE is said to have been the last Red Man
In Acton. And the Miller is said to have laughed —
If you like to call such a sound a laugh.
But he gave no one else a laugher's license.
For he turned suddenly grave as if to say,
"Whose business,— if I take it on myself,
Whose business — but why talk round the barn? —
When it's just that I hold with getting a thing done with."
You can't get back and see it as he saw it.
It's too long a story to go into now.
You'd have to have been there and lived it.
Then you wouldn't have looked on it as just a matter
Of who began it between the two races.

Some guttural exclamation of surprise
The Red Man gave in poking about the mill
Over the great big thumping shuffling mill-stone
Disgusted the Miller physically as coming
From one who had no right to be heard from.
"Come, John," he said, "you want to see the wheel pit?"

He took him down below a cramping rafter,
And showed him, through a manhole in the floor,
The water in desperate straits like frantic fish,
Salmon and sturgeon, lashing with their tails.
Then he shut down the trap door with a ring in it
That jangled even above the general noise,

And came up stairs alone — and gave that laugh,
And said something to a man with a meal-sack
That the man with the meal-sack didn't catch — then.
Oh, yes, he showed John the wheel pit all right.

SNOW

THE three stood listening to a fresh access
Of wind that caught against the house a moment,
Gulped snow, and then blew free again — the Coles
Dressed, but dishevelled from some hours of sleep,
Meserve belittled in the great skin coat he wore.

Meserve was first to speak. He pointed backward
Over his shoulder with his pipe-stem, saying,
"You can just see it glancing off the roof
Making a great scroll upward toward the sky,
Long enough for recording all our names on.—
I think I'll just call up my wife and tell her
I'm here — so far — and starting on again.
I'll call her softly so that if she's wise
And gone to sleep, she needn't wake to answer."
Three times he barely stirred the bell, then listened.
"Why, Lett, still up? Lett, I'm at Cole's. I'm late.
I called you up to say Good-night from here
Before I went to say Good-morning there.—
I thought I would.— I know, but, Lett — I know —
I could, but what's the sense? The rest won't be
So bad.— Give me an hour for it.— Ho, ho,
Three hours to here! But that was all up hill;
The rest is down.— Why no, no, not a wallow:
They kept their heads and took their time to it
Like darlings, both of them. They're in the barn.—
My dear, I'm coming just the same. I didn't
Call you to ask you to invite me home.—"
He lingered for some word she wouldn't say,

Said it at last himself, "Good-night," and then,
Getting no answer, closed the telephone.
The three stood in the lamplight round the table
With lowered eyes a moment till he said,
"I'll just see how the horses are."

"Yes, do,"

Both the Coles said together. Mrs. Cole
Added: "You can judge better after seeing.—
I want you here with me, Fred. Leave him here,
Brother Meserve. You know to find your way
Out through the shed."

"I guess I know my way,

I guess I know where I can find my name
Carved in the shed to tell me who I am
If it don't tell me where I am. I used
To play—"

"You tend your horses and come back.

Fred Cole, you're going to let him!"

"Well, aren't you?

How can you help yourself?"

"I called him Brother.

Why did I call him that?"

"It's right enough.

That's all you ever heard him called round here.
He seems to have lost off his Christian name."

"Christian enough I should call that myself.
He took no notice, did he? Well, at least
I didn't use it out of love of him,

The dear knows. I detest the thought of him
With his ten children under ten years old.
I hate his wretched little Racker Sect,
All's ever I heard of it, which isn't much.
But that's not saying — Look, Fred Cole, it's twelve,
Isn't it, now? He's been here half an hour.
He says he left the village store at nine.
Three hours to do four miles — a mile an hour
Or not much better. Why, it doesn't seem
As if a man could move that slow and move.
Try to think what he did with all that time.
And three miles more to go!"

"Don't let him go.
Stick to him, Helen. Make him answer you.
That sort of man talks straight on all his life
From the last thing he said himself, stone deaf
To anything anyone else may say.
I should have thought, though, you could make him hear
you."

"What is he doing out a night like this?
Why can't he stay at home?"

"He had to preach."

"It's no night to be out."

"He may be small,
He may be good, but one thing's sure, he's tough."

"And strong of stale tobacco."

"He'll pull through.'

"You only say so. Not another house
Or shelter to put into from this place
To theirs. I'm going to call his wife again."

"Wait and he may. Let's see what he will do.
Let's see if he will think of her again.
But then I doubt he's thinking of himself
He doesn't look on it as anything."

"He shan't go — there!"

"It *is* a night, my dear."

"One thing: he didn't drag God into it."

"He don't consider it a case for God."

"You think so, do you? You don't know the kind.
He's getting up a miracle this minute.
Privately — to himself, right now, he's thinking
He'll make a case of it if he succeeds,
But keep still if he fails."

"Keep still all over.
He'll be dead — dead and buried."

"Such a trouble!
Not but I've every reason not to care
What happens to him if it only takes
Some of the sanctimonious conceit
Out of one of those pious scalawags."

"Nonsense to that! You want to see him safe."

"You like the runt."

"Don't you a little?"

"Well,
I don't like what he's doing, which is what
You like, and like him for."

"Oh, yes you do.
You like your fun as well as anyone;
Only you women have to put these airs on
To impress men. You've got us so ashamed
Of being men we can't look at a good fight
Between two boys and not feel bound to stop it.
Let the man freeze an ear or two, I say.—
He's here. I leave him all to you. Go in
And save his life.— All right, come in, Meserve.
Sit down, sit down. How did you find the horses?"

"Fine, fine."

"And ready for some more? My wife here
Says it won't do. You've got to give it up."

"Won't you to please me? Please! If I say please?
Mr. Meserve, I'll leave it to *your* wife.
What *did* your wife say on the telephone?"

Meserve seemed to heed nothing but the lamp
Or something not far from it on the table.
By straightening out and lifting a forefinger,
He pointed with his hand from where it lay
Like a white crumpled spider on his knee:
"That leaf there in your open book! It moved
Just then, I thought. It's stood erect like that,
There on the table, ever since I came,
Trying to turn itself backward or forward,
I've had my eye on it to make out which;
If forward, then it's with a friend's impatience—

You see I know — to get you on to things
It wants to see how you will take, if backward
It's from regret for something you have passed
And failed to see the good of. Never mind,
Things must expect to come in front of us
A many times — I don't say just how many —
That varies with the things — before we see them.
One of the lies would make it out that nothing
Ever presents itself before us twice.
Where would we be at last if that were so?
Our very life depends on everything's
Recurring till we answer from within.
The thousandth time may prove the charm.— That leaf!
It can't turn either way. It needs the wind's help.
But the wind didn't move it if it moved.
It moved itself. The wind's at naught in here.
It couldn't stir so sensitively poised
A thing as that. It couldn't reach the lamp
To get a puff of black smoke from the flame,
Or blow a rumple in the collie's coat.
You make a little foursquare block of air,
Quiet and light and warm, in spite of all
The illimitable dark and cold and storm,
And by so doing give these three, lamp, dog,
And book-leaf, that keep near you, their repose;
Though for all anyone can tell, repose
May be the thing you haven't, yet you give it.
So false it is that what we haven't we can't give;
So false, that what we always say is true.
I'll have to turn the leaf if no one else will.
It won't lie down. Then let it stand. Who cares?"

"I shouldn't want to hurry you, Meserve,
But if you're going — Say you'll stay, you know?
But let me raise this curtain on a scene,

And show you how it's piling up against you.
You see the snow-white through the white of frost?
Ask Helen how far up the sash it's climbed
Since last we read the gage."

"It looks as if
Some pallid thing had squashed its features flat
And its eyes shut with overeagerness
To see what people found so interesting
In one another, and had gone to sleep
Of its own stupid lack of understanding,
Or broken its white neck of mushroom stuff
Short off, and died against the window-pane."

"Brother Meserve, take care, you'll scare yourself
More than you will us with such nightmare talk.
It's you it matters to, because it's you
Who have to go out into it alone."

"Let him talk, Helen, and perhaps he'll stay."

"Before you drop the curtain — I'm reminded:
You recollect the boy who came out here
To breathe the air one winter — had a room
Down at the Averys'? Well, one sunny morning
After a downy storm, he passed our place
And found me banking up the house with snow.
And I was burrowing in deep for warmth,
Piling it well above the window-sills.
The snow against the window caught his eye.
'Hey, that's a pretty thought'— those were his words.
'So you can think it's six feet deep outside,
While you sit warm and read up balanced rations.
You can't get too much winter in the winter.'
Those were his words. And he went home and all

But banked the daylight out of Avery's windows.
Now you and I would go to no such length.
At the same time you can't deny it makes
It not a mite worse, sitting here, we three,
Playing our fancy, to have the snowline run
So high across the pane outside. There where
There is a sort of tunnel in the frost
More like a tunnel than a hole — way down
At the far end of it you see a stir
And quiver like the frayed edge of the drift
Blown in the wind. I *like* that — I like *that*.
Well, now I leave you, people."

"Come, Meserve,
We thought you were deciding not to go —
The ways you found to say the praise of comfort
And being where you are. You want to stay."

"I'll own it's cold for such a fall of snow.
This house is frozen brittle, all except
This room you sit in. If you think the wind
Sounds further off, it's not because it's dying;
You're further under in the snow — that's all —
And feel it less. Hear the soft bombs of dust
It bursts against us at the chimney mouth,
And at the eaves. I like it from inside
More than I shall out in it. But the horses
Are rested and it's time to say good-night,
And let you get to bed again. Good-night,
Sorry I had to break in on your sleep."

"Lucky for you you did. Lucky for you
You had us for a half-way station
To stop at. If you were the kind of man
Paid heed to women, you'd take my advice
And for your family's sake stay where you are.

But what good is my saying it over and over?
You've done more than you had a right to think
You could do — *now.* You know the risk you take
In going on."

"Our snow-storms as a rule
Aren't looked on as man-killers, and although
I'd rather be the beast that sleeps the sleep
Under it all, his door sealed up and lost,
Than the man fighting it to keep above it,
Yet think of the small birds at roost and not
In nests. Shall I be counted less than they are?
Their bulk in water would be frozen rock
In no time out to-night. And yet to-morrow
They will come budding boughs from tree to tree
Flirting their wings and saying Chickadee,
As if not knowing what you meant by the word storm."

"But why when no one wants you to go on?
Your wife — she doesn't want you to. We don't,
And you yourself don't want to. Who else is there?"

"Save us from being cornered by a woman.
Well, there's"— She told Fred afterward that in
The pause right there, she thought the dreaded word
Was coming, "God." But no, he only said
"Well, there's — the storm. That says I must go on.
That wants me as a war might if it came.
Ask any man."

He threw her that as something
To last her till he got outside the door.
He had Cole with him to the barn to see him off.
When Cole returned he found his wife still standing
Beside the table near the open book,
Not reading it.

"Well, what kind of a man
Do you call that?" she said.

"He had the gift
Of words, or is it tongues, I ought to say?"

"Was ever such a man for seeing likeness?"

"Or disregarding people's civil questions —
What? We've found out in one hour more about him
Than we had seeing him pass by in the road
A thousand times. If that's the way he preaches!
You didn't think you'd keep him after all.
Oh, I'm not blaming you. He didn't leave you
Much say in the matter, and I'm just as glad
We're not in for a night of him. No sleep
If he had stayed. The least thing set him going.
It's quiet as an empty church without him."

"But how much better off are we as it is?
We'll have to sit here till we know he's safe."

"Yes, I suppose you'll want to, but I shouldn't.
He knows what he can do, or he wouldn't try.
Get into bed I say, and get some rest.
He won't come back, and if he telephones,
It won't be for an hour or two."

"Well then.
We can't be any help by sitting here
And living his fight through with him, I suppose."

Cole had been telephoning in the dark.

Mrs. Cole's voice came from an inner room:
"Did she call you or you call her?"

"She me.
You'd better dress: you won't go back to bed.
We must have been asleep: it's three and after."

"Had she been ringing long? I'll get my wrapper.
I want to speak to her."

"All she said was,
He hadn't come and had he really started."

"She knew he had, poor thing, two hours ago."

"He had the shovel. He'll have made a fight."

"Why did I ever let him leave this house!"

"Don't begin that. You did the best you could
To keep him — though perhaps you didn't quite
Conceal a wish to see him show the spunk
To disobey you. Much his wife'll thank you."

"Fred, after all I said! You shan't make out
That it was any way but what it was.
Did she let on by any word she said
She didn't thank me?"

"When I told her 'Gone,'
'Well then,' she said, and 'Well then'— like a threat.
And then her voice came scraping slow: 'Oh, you,
Why did you let him go'?"

"Asked why we let him?
You let me there. I'll ask her why she let him.
She didn't dare to speak when he was here.

Their number's — twenty-one? The thing won't work.
Someone's receiver's down. The handle stumbles.

The stubborn thing, the way it jars your arm!
It's theirs. She's dropped it from her hand and gone."

"Try speaking. Say 'Hello'!"

"Hello. Hello."

"What do you hear?"

"I hear an empty room —
You know — it sounds that way. And yes, I hear —
I think I hear a clock — and windows rattling.
No step though. If she's there she's sitting down."

"Shout, she may hear you."

"Shouting is no good."

"Keep speaking then."

"Hello. Hello. Hello.
You don't suppose —? She wouldn't go out doors?"

"I'm half afraid that's just what she might do."

"And leave the children?"

"Wait and call again.
You can't hear whether she has left the door
Wide open and the wind's blown out the lamp
And the fire's died and the room's dark and cold?"

"One of two things, either she's gone to bed
Or gone out doors."

"In which case both are lost.
Do you know what she's like? Have you ever met her?
It's strange she doesn't want to speak to us."

"Fred, see if you can hear what I hear. Come."

"A clock maybe."

"Don't you hear something else?"

"Not talking."

"No."

"Why, yes, I hear — what is it?"

"What do you say it is?"

"A baby's crying!
Frantic it sounds, though muffled and far off."

"Its mother wouldn't let it cry like that,
Not if she's there."

"What do you make of it?"

"There's only one thing possible to make,
That is, assuming — that she has gone out.
Of course she hasn't though." They both sat down
Helpless. "There's nothing we can do till morning."

"Fred, I shan't let you think of going out."

"Hold on." The double bell began to chirp.
They started up. Fred took the telephone.
"Hello, Meserve. You're there, then! — And your wife?

Good! Why I asked — she didn't seem to answer.
He says she went to let him in the barn.—
We're glad. Oh, say no more about it, man.
Drop in and see us when you're passing."

"Well,
She has him then, though what she wants him for
I *don't* see."

"Possibly not for herself.
Maybe she only wants him for the children."

"The whole to-do seems to have been for nothing.
What spoiled our night was to him just his fun.
What did he come in for? — To talk and visit?
Thought he'd just call to tell us it was snowing.
If he thinks he is going to make our house
A halfway coffee house 'twixt town and nowhere ——"

"I thought you'd feel you'd been too much concerned."

"You think you haven't been concerned yourself."

"If you mean he was inconsiderate
To rout us out to think for him at midnight
And then take our advice no more than nothing,
Why, I agree with you. But let's forgive him.
We've had a share in one night of his life.
What'll you bet he ever calls again?"

THE SOUND OF THE TREES

I wonder about the trees.
Why do we wish to bear
Forever the noise of these
More than another noise
So close to our dwelling place?
We suffer them by the day
Till we lose all measure of pace,
And fixity in our joys,
And acquire a listening air.
They are that that talks of going
But never gets away;
And that talks no less for knowing,
As it grows wiser and older,
That now it means to stay.
My feet tug at the floor
And my head sways to my shoulder
Sometimes when I watch trees sway,
From the window or the door.
I shall set forth for somewhere,
I shall make the reckless choice
Some day when they are in voice
And tossing so as to scare
The white clouds over them on.
I shall have less to say,
But I shall be gone.